Princesses,
Mermaids & Fairies
Coloring Book

Lynnda Rakos

DOVER PUBLICATIONS, INC.
Mineola, New York

Explore an enchanting fantasy world where lovely princesses reign and sprightly fairies play with magical dust. In this book of thirty black-and-white illustrations, you will also find a mermaid riding a sea horse, a princess with her playful poodle, and fairies cavorting in teacups. Color in these charming scenes with crayons, markers, or colored pencils and find yourself swept away to fairy tale land!

Bibliographical Note
Princesses, Mermaids and Fairies Coloring Book is a new work, first published by Dover Publications, Inc., in 2012.

International Standard Book Number
ISBN-13: 978-0-486-48664-2
ISBN-10: 0-486-48664-8

Manufactured in the United States by LSC Communications
undefined
www.doverpublications.com